This Walker book belongs to:

....

....

NANETTE'S BAGUETTE

words and pictures by
Mo Willems

Today is a day Nanette won't soon forget.

Today,
in the kitchenette,
Mum tells Nanette
that Nanette gets
to get the baguette!

Baguettes are warm.

Baguettes smell wonderful.

Getting to get the baguette is Nanette's biggest responsibility yet.

Is Nanette set to get the baguette?

But on the way ...

Nanette sees
Georgette!

And Suzette!

And Bret
(with his clarinet)!

Look!

There's Mr Barnett
with his pet,
Antoinette!

Nanette pets Antoinette.

Did Nanette forget the baguette?

"Gotta jet! I've got a baguette to get," says Nanette to the quartet.

Baker Juliette has met Nanette.

She knows it is Nanette's first baguette get.

So, Juliette gets Nanette the best baguette yet!

Nanette! Did you get the baguette?

The baguette is still warm.

The baguette still tastes wonderful.

(And there still is some of it...)

Can Nanette stop tasting the baguette?

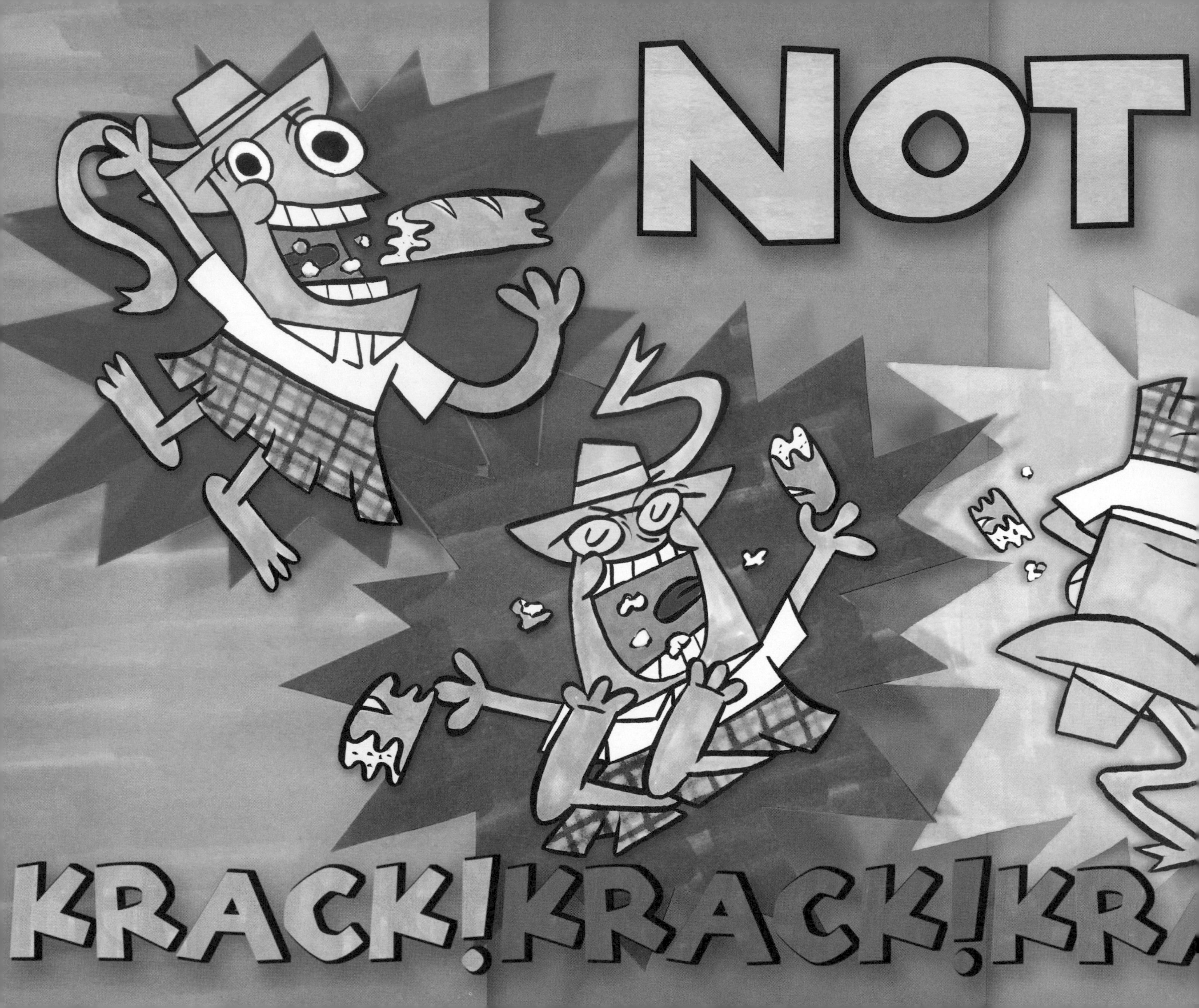
NOT
KRACK!KRACK!

There is no
more baguette!

Nanette begins
to fret.

Will Mum be upset?

WILL MUM REGRET SHE LET NANETTE GET THE BAGUETTE?

Now Nanette is wet.

Wet with no baguette.

This is as bad as it can get.

Nanette wishes Mum had never let Nanette get that baguette!

Maybe Nanette will move to Tibet.

Tibet is as far away as you can get.

Nanette would need a jet.

Can Nanette go home instead?

Can Nanette face her mum?

What will she do?

"Where is the baguette, Nanette?" asks Mum. "Did you forget?"

Nanette did not forget.

Nanette is upset.

Nanette is beset with regret.

She sweats.

I ATE THE BAGUETTE!

Mum hugs Nanette.

It is warm.

It is wonderful.

(Like a million baguettes.)

"The day's not over, yet, Nanette," says Mum. "Let's reset!"

Baker Juliette is surprised to see Nanette.

(But not too surprised.)

Nanette's mum gets another baguette.

Now they are all set –
Mum,
Nanette,
and a baguette.

The baguette is warm.
The baguette smells wonderful...

Today is a day Nanette won't soon forget!

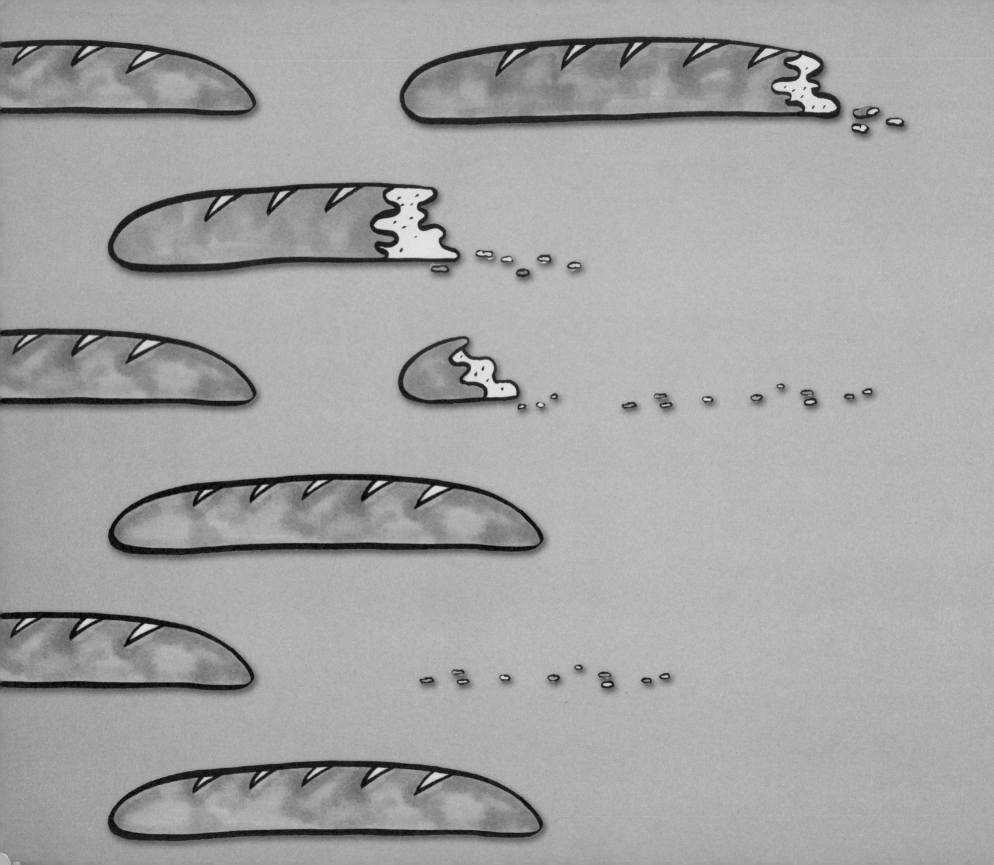

To Trixie Willems –

for showing me what it's all about

The images in this story are comprised of photographed handcrafted cardboard-and-paper constructions digitally integrated with photographed illustrations and additions.

Special thanks to Angela DiTerlizzi for sharing her photographic equipment, Cher Willems for her help and enthusiasm, and the patrons of Amanda's Boot Camp for their generous (and copious) supply of toilet paper and paper-towel rolls.

First published in Great Britain 2017 by Walker Books Ltd
87 Vauxhall Walk, London SE11 5HJ

2 4 6 8 10 9 7 5 3 1

The right of Mo Willems to be identified as author/illustrator of this work has been asserted by him in accordance with the Copyright, Designs and Patents Act 1988

First published in the United States 2016 by Hyperion Books for Children, an imprint of Disney Book Group.
British publication rights arranged with Wernick & Pratt Agency, LLC.

This book has been typeset in Bryant Pro Medium

Printed in China

British Library Cataloguing in Publication Data:
a catalogue record for this book is available from the British Library

ISBN 978-1-4063-7621-0

www.walker.co.uk

WALKER BOOKS
AND SUBSIDIARIES
LONDON • BOSTON • SYDNEY • AUCKLAND

Mo Willems

Mo Willems is a three-time Caldecott Honor winner for *Don't Let the Pigeon Drive the Bus!*, *Knuffle Bunny: A Cautionary Tale* and *Knuffle Bunny Too: A Case of Mistaken Identity*. His books have been translated into over 25 languages, and his celebrated *Elephant & Piggie* early-reader series has been awarded the Theodor Seuss Geisel Medal on two occasions as well as five Honors. Other favourites include *That Is Not a Good Idea!* and *Goldilocks and the Three Dinosaurs*. Before he turned to children's books, Mo was a writer and animator on *Sesame Street*, where he won six Emmy Awards. Mo lives with his family in Massachusetts, USA.

Find him online at www.mowillems.com and on Twitter as @The_Pigeon.

978-1-84428-513-6

978-1-84428-545-7

978-1-4063-0812-9

978-1-4063-1550-9

978-1-4063-4009-9

978-1-4063-5778-3

978-1-4063-5558-1

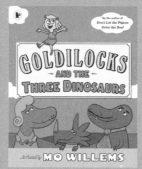
978-1-4063-5532-1

978-1-4063-1215-7

978-1-4063-4731-9

978-1-84428-059-9

978-1-4063-1382-6

978-1-4063-3649-8

Available from all good booksellers

www.walker.co.uk